THE
LOST
CITY

by

ROGER HURN AND JANE A.C. WEST

Illustrated by Stik

Tribe
Books

To Eve – for always showing me the way.

With special thanks to:

Jack Bradley

First published in 2011 in Great Britain by
Barrington Stoke Ltd
18 Walker St, Edinburgh, EH3 7LP

www.barringtonstoke.co.uk

ISBN: 978-1-84299-604-1

Printed in China by Leo

The publisher gratefully acknowledges support from the Scottish Arts
Council towards the publication of this title.

Scottish
Arts Council

WHO ARE TRIBE?

ARE THEY HUMANS?

OR ARE THEY ANIMALS?

Tribe are humans *and* animals.

They are super-heroes with special powers.

They can *shape-shift* – change from animals to humans and back again.

THEIR PLAN: to save the world from anyone who tries to destroy it.

Tribe need to find the bad guys – before it's too late.

The Earth is in trouble – and only Tribe have the power to help.

Tribe are helped by TOK – the Tree Of Knowledge.

Tribe can travel all over the world using the roots of trees.

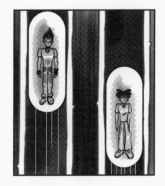

Tribe also have the power to talk to animals – and they can send each other mind-messages, even when they are miles apart.

CAST LIST

Finn

Bruin

Kat

Mo

Talon

Vana

and ...

Rich Moneybags!

Contents

1   The Lost City   1

2   Snakes Alive!   6

3   The Keepers of the Lost City   12

4   Yaguara   18

5   Splash and Grab   25

    Fun Stuff!   40

Chapter 1
The Lost City

The Tree Of Knowledge (TOK), the huge oak tree that was Tribe's secret Head Quarters, was shaking. A message had come through the root system. TOK's eyes snapped open. "Wake up, Tribe!" he snapped.

Finn, Bruin, Vana, Talon, Mo and Kat jumped up and down with excitement. They knew that TOK was about to send them off on a new mission.

"What's up, TOK?" asked Finn. "Who needs Tribe's help this time?"

"Willy Maykit, the explorer. He has vanished in the Amazon jungle. He set off from a village called Napo three months ago. He's trying to find the Lost City of Gold."

"Then that's where we'll start looking for him," said Vana.

"But we don't know where the Lost City is," said Bruin. "It's lost."

"Doh," said Vana. "I know that! What I mean is that we must *start* at Napo!"

"So what are we waiting for?" said Talon. "Let's go!"

"Not so fast," said Kat. "I've got to grab my umbrella first."

"Why?" asked Bruin.

"Because cats don't like to get wet," said Kat. "And in the rain forest it rains every day."

"Wow," said Finn. "That's a lot of rain – and no one likes a soggy moggy!"

5

Chapter 2
Snakes Alive!

Tribe were standing in an open patch of rain forest. The air was hot and steamy.

"It really is wet in this jungle," said Finn. "I'm getting soaked."

"Yes," replied Bruin. "But that's not rain – it's the monkeys in the trees above your head having fun."

Finn looked up and a wet stream of wee splashed down onto his face. The monkeys screeched with delight. Finn didn't.

"Gross!" said Kat. "I'm so glad I brought my brolly."

Mo squeaked in alarm as a huge snake swung down from a branch and began to wrap itself around her. Bruin morphed into a bear, grabbed the scaly serpent's tail and tugged hard. Mo spun round as the shocked snake suddenly let go its grip and found itself face to face with a very fierce grizzly bear.

"I've always wanted a real snake-skin tie," said Bruin with an evil grin.

The snake hissed at him. "Oh, don't get *hiss*-terical," Bruin added. "I'm only joking." He dropped the snake and it slithered away at top speed.

"Thanks," said Mo. "I think that snake had a *crush* on me!"

"Well, it's gone off to have a hissy fit now," replied Bruin. "But the jungle is full of dangers like that, so watch out."

Just then a band of Amazon Indians stepped out from behind the trees. Their faces were painted to look like jaguars and each man had a blow pipe loaded with a poison dart. They were pointing their blow pipes at Tribe!

Chapter 3
The Keepers of the Lost City

"Don't panic, these chaps mean you no harm." A tall thin man dressed in a ragged safari suit walked up to them. The men lowered their deadly blow pipes.

"Hey, you're Willy Maykit," said Talon. "We've been looking for you."

"And now you've found me," replied the

explorer. "And not a moment too soon."

Vana snarled. "Have these Indians kidnapped you?"

"No – they saved my life. I was bitten by a deadly spider. My Indian friends rescued me just in time."

"So why do you need our help?" asked Kat.

"Because these Indians guard the Lost City of Gold. They took me there to cure me when I was sick. But we were followed by the evil agents of Rich Moneybags."

Talon groaned. "Oh, no. Rich Moneybags is the richest man in the world. And he is as bad as a shark with tooth-ache."

"That's right. He knew I was trying to find the Lost City, so he sent his men after me. Now he knows where it is, and he's going to steal the gold!"

"But won't the Indians stop him?" said Mo.

Willy Maykit's face was sad. "They've no chance against men with guns."

The Indian warriors began to chant and point at Tribe.

"What are they saying?" asked Bruin.

"These Indians are called the Jaguar people. They believe that some humans can take on the shape of animals. They saw you change into a bear. They say that you can use your magic powers to defeat the bad men."

"Well, they're right," said Bruin. "Come on, guys, we've got a Lost City of Gold to save."

Chapter 4
Yaguara

The Lost City was in a hidden valley deep in the jungle. A small river curled round it like a cat's tail. Tribe and their new friends watched from the jungle as men loaded chests full of stolen gold onto canoes moored at the river bank.

A large helicopter came down from the clear blue sky and landed by the edge of the river. Rich Moneybags jumped out from the helicopter and began shouting orders at his men. They ran off, but soon returned carrying a large statue of a jaguar made of solid gold. The Indians groaned and shook their fists in fury.

"That statue is the most important thing in the world to the Jaguar people," said Willy Maykit. "They believe that if it leaves the City, the place will crumble and they will die."

"That is not going to happen," said Kat. "I may not be a jaguar, but I'm still a fully paid up member of the cat family."

She morphed into a cat, then screeched as if her tail was in a steel trap. In answer to her call, a sleek and powerful jaguar burst out of the jungle. It prowled over to her. The Indians gasped.

"Meet my cousin. The Indians call him

'the beast who kills with one bite'. I call him

Yag."

The jaguar opened its jaws. Sunlight glinted off its sharp teeth.

"Stop showing off, Yag," said Kat. "We've got some hunting to do." She jumped up onto the jaguar's broad back and Yag slipped back into the forest with her, a silent as a shadow.

Chapter 5
Splash and Grab

"Kat isn't the only one with family around here," said Finn. He raced off and dived into the river. When he shot up, he was at the head of a pod of Amazon River dolphins.

They powered towards the gold-filled canoes. The dolphins grabbed the tow ropes in their teeth and swam away with the canoes.

The watching Indians cheered and Vana and Mo high-fived each other. "Finn's just done a *splash* and grab raid!" said Mo. "But where's Bruin?"

"There!" said eagle-eyed Talon, pointing down into the Lost City. "He's about to get to grips with Rich Moneybags."

Bruin was lumbering towards the crazy crook, but he was too far away to stop him. Rich Moneybags yelled at his men. "Hurry up, you fools. Stash the statue away in the helicopter while I take care of the bear!"

He pulled out a gun and took aim at Bruin. Bruin froze. He knew Moneybags couldn't miss. The billionaire grinned. "Hey, you're not a bear – you're a sitting duck," he said.

But before he could pull the trigger a large jaguar and a not so small cat landed on top of him like a ton of furry bricks.

Rich Moneybags' men dropped the gold statue. They ran for their lives as the Indian warriors, led by a snarling wolf and a screaming eagle with a very small mouse on its back, came charging at them from out of the jungle. Yag and Kat leapt off Rich Moneybags and joined in the chase.

Rich Moneybags crawled towards the helicopter to make his escape. "Oh, no you don't," yelled Bruin. He hurled himself at the helicopter and sent it crashing into the river. The pilot scrambled free and swam off as fast as he could while the helicopter sank.

Yag pounced on Rich Moneybags again.

"That was close, Bruin," said Kat. "If Yag and I hadn't arrived when we did, Rich Moneybags would have turned you into a *polo* bear."

"What's a polo bear?" asked Bruin.

"A bear with a hole in the middle," said Kat.

"So what are we going to do with him?"

Yag looked at Rich Moneybags and licked his lips. Kat grinned. "Well, we could ..."

"No, we couldn't," said Mo firmly. "Willy Maykit and the Indians will take Mr Moneybags out of the rainforest and hand him over to the police."

"But then he'll know the way back to the Lost City," said Kat, shaking her head.

"Not if the Indians blind-fold him first," said Mo.

"And his helicopter and its satnav are at the bottom of the river," said Bruin. "So the Lost City is safe."

Kat's eyes glittered coldly for a second, but then she smiled. "OK," she agreed. "Anyway, I guess old Moneybags would be too *rich* a meal for Yag!"

AMAZON INDIANS – A VANISHING WAY OF LIFE

500 years ago, 10,000,000 Indians lived in the Amazon rain forest. Now there are fewer than 200,000. And the way of life of these last Indian tribes is at risk. Logging companies are cutting down the trees and building roads across the Indians' land.

Mining companies dig up the earth, pollute the rivers and kill the fish. They frighten the animals away, making it much harder for the Indians to hunt for food. Farmers burn down the forest so they can put their cattle on the cleared land.

The Indians have lived in the rain forest for thousands of years and know its plants and animals. We have so much we can learn from them, but we are in danger of destroying the forest and its people forever before we have found out all that they know.

To find out more about the tribes who live in the Amazon rain forest go to: www.amazon-indians.org/.

KAT - CAT GiRL

CAN BE A BIT, WELL, CATTY.
LIKES TO BE ON HER OWN.

SPECIAL SKILL: always lands on her feet, no matter how far she falls.

LOVES: being warm, sleeping in the sun.

HATES: water, travelling by TOK's tree root system and mice.

MOST LIKELY TO SAY: "Well, wash my whiskers!"

BIGGEST SECRET: doesn't really feel part of Tribe.

TRIBE TALK!

To:	Kat
From:	Charlotte
Subject:	Save the Rain forest

Hi Kat,

How can I help save the rainforest?

Charlotte

To:	Charlotte
From:	Kat
Subject:	Re: Save the Rain forest

Hi Charlotte!

Why not raise money with your friends and family? You can give the money to a charity such as The Rainforest Foundation UK that works to protect and look after rain forests.

More power to your paws,

Kat

FYI: JAGUARS

• Jaguars are so sleek and beautiful they have had a famous luxury sports car named after them.

• Jaguars look very like leopards – but jaguars are bigger and stronger.

- The jaguar is the top predator in South America.

- A jaguar often kills its prey with one big bite through its skull.

- Jaguars climb trees but, unlike most cats, they like swimming.

- The only creatures that are a threat to the jaguar are human beings.

JOKE OF THE DAY

KAT: What looks like half a cat?

VANA: I don't know...

KAT: The other half!